Without the Confines

of

My Rhymes

By

Xtina Marie

A HellBound Books LLC Publication
Copyright © 2018 by HellBound Books Publishing
LLC
All Rights Reserved

Cover and art design by Luke Spooner

for
HellBound Books Publishing LLC

www.hellboundbookspublishing.com

Printed in the United States of America

Contents:

Acknowledgements:

I am a rhymer. I've *always* been a
rhymer. In fact, I would have told you
that I just didn't get free verse poetry.
Then I read *Ruin My Lipstick by R.B.
O'Brien*. And never looked back.

Thanks to Denise Jury for always
catching my booboos.

Shout out to Luke Spooner for my
beautiful cover.

And a special thank you to the beau,
the inspiration behind many of the
poems in Without <3

Evenings Like This

Enjoying
an evening
doing nothing
but listening to the
nonsense
of my loved ones.
She's gaming.
What game- I'm never sure.
He's reading aloud
from a book,
a part he finds
particularly humorous.
I can hear
the neighborhood dogs
randomly bark,
and some children
doing what children do
at the playground
a block away.
In a few short weeks
it'll be summer
and I'll enjoy
evenings like this

every night.

I'm Home

My favorite sound
will always be
your voice.
It cradles me
like a warm blanket
that I pull close
on a cold
winter's night.
It surrounds me
like the soothing water
from the bubble bath
as I unwind
from a trying day.
I call it to mind
as easy as I
call to mind
my own name.
I hear it
and immediately
I'm home.

Thinking Back

Thinking back
to what was;
hot and heavy,
crazy lust.
This need, this desire
most addicting.
Frenzied, blurry vision,
my thoughts, you only
always.
My body responding
to your every word,
every whisper
in my ear.
Now here we are,
a few years later.
Older. Wiser.
Settled in.
Comfortable.
Habits established.
I wear you

like I wear
my favorite t-shirt.
The grey one,
that's faded some
with time.
But still
my thoughts, you only
always.

Xtina Marie

We Both Know

We joke about
baseball.
You say I love
the Blue Jays
a bit more than you.
I laugh at your
silliness.
We both know
you're the beating
of my heart
and the blood
in my veins.

Your Name

I cried the night
we said goodbye.
The sobs
wracked my body
and my eyes
burned with too many tears.
My heart hurt,
a pain I doubted
would ever go away.
The next morning
I felt empty
because a part of me
was missing.
Would I ever
be whole again?
It's been years now,
too many to count.
And still, I flinch
when someone says
your name.

Xtina Marie

Sometimes

Sometimes
I lie in bed
and stare at your
picture.
Tracing
every angle
of your face
with my eyes.
Sometimes
I play back the
voicemail
you left me,
your deep voice
so familiar,
echoing
in my head
just because.
Sometimes
when we're
talking
I whisper

"I love you"
out of the
blue
taking you by
surprise.
Sometimes
my heart soars
with just
the mere
thought of you.
Sometimes.

Xtina Marie

Years Past

Melancholy
is my name today.
The birds are chirping,
children playing
in the sun.
Smiling, cheerful.
And I want to cry.
Why?
I haven't the answer.
I find my thoughts
drifting
to years past.
Remembering
people I used to know.
I haven't thought of him
in so long.
And I panic,
thinking what if
someday
you become
someone I haven't thought of
in years.

Already Gone

I stared through the lens
of my camera
frozen.
He lay sleeping,
one hand under his cheek,
the other flung
over the side of the couch.
His breathing deep.
Soft snores
here and there.
So handsome.
Beautiful even.
He doesn't realize
my heart beats
to the rhythm of
the blood in his veins.
I wanted to
preserve this moment.
Freeze time.
Capture it.
So that it could
never be forgotten.
But then I blinked.

And the moment
was already
gone.

And Yet

I know
you know
when your words
sting.
And yet you say them
anyway.
Hearing
the hurt
in my voice,
seeing
the pain
in my eyes
and yet you
pretend
not to notice.

Xtina Marie

Sundays

Sundays were made
for sleeping in
and messy hair.
Watching the baseball game
in pajamas
while you order takeout.
For long talks about nothing,
lying side by side
in bed
staring at the ceiling
while we laugh,
finding joy in everything.
For board games and
movie marathons
and holding hands
while we steal kisses
here and there.
For smoldering looks and
fevered pulses
while we slowly peel away
our clothes
in the same fashion
we would peel away

the stress of the week.

Xtina Marie

His Mama's Boy

(written on Mother's Day 2018)

He's his own
person;
never following
the crowd.
He likes jazz
and old pocket watches,
sports an afro
but wears a tie.
He's quiet
but loud,
insanely smart
and crazy for cats.
It took him
forever
to say his first word
and said it was
because
he was waiting 'til he knew
all the words.
He's sensitive
but strong
and I hope he'll

always be
his mama's boy.

Xtina Marie

She Calls Me Mommy

(written on Mother's Day 2018)

She's loud
and abrasive
while being
sensitive and sweet.
Always so excitable
or bored to tears,
never an in
between.
She's beautiful
and unique,
not caring
what anyone thinks.
So damn
opinionated
while being forgiving
to a fault.
She'll always be my
best friend,
like she's been
since she learned

to walk.
And still, she calls me
Mommy.

Xtina Marie

Wine-Colored Glasses

Deciding to write
wearing my wine-colored
glasses
with the slight hint
of peach
swirling around
my tongue.
I lick my lips
and take another
long sip
while I think the things
I know I wouldn't,
were it not for
my wine-colored
glasses.
Like how I laugh off
your little digs
that I'm sure you know
sting.
Or how
it wouldn't be me
who'd end up
regretting

a hasty decision
made while wearing
my wine-colored
glasses.

Xtina Marie

Reality

Anticipating
tonight
when our eyes meet
and you know
exactly
what I want.
What I desire.
Your touch
still makes me
shiver
and I crave
your lips
that seek out
the nape of my neck
as I tilt my head
waiting to feel
your teeth grazing
my skin.
I grow
feverish.
Excited.
Aroused.
My breath catching

wondering when
my anticipation
will become
reality.

Xtina Marie

Trash or Treasure

How to decipher
the trash
from the
treasure?
There should be some
definite answer here.
Some sort of measure.
But there isn't.
And so we pray.
We hope.
The same words
that speak
so loudly,
the same thoughts
that float
so tangibly
speak to others.

Intoxication

Soft moans
getting louder,
more frenzied.
Sweat building
on glistening bodies
overheated with
passion, need, lust, love.
Gasping your name
as I release
yet again.
Drunk on you.
Dizzy, heady
intoxication
drowning me
but I gladly
surrendered
long ago.

Xtina Marie

The Storm

The sky
darkens.
Mirroring
my mood.
Negativity
swirling,
spinning
as the
wind picks up.
Tree branches
snap, break, scatter,
my mind
snapping, breaking, scattering.
Finally
the rains
begin.
Cleansing, soothing.
I breathe
and feel
the tears on my cheeks;
cleansing, soothing
and I know
when the clouds

part
and the sun
escapes—
so soon
forgetting
the havoc
of moments before—
a smile will
escape my lips;
full, shining, brilliant.
And I will move on
until
the next storm.

Xtina Marie

My Everything

He is my
first thought
before my eyes
focus.
He's with me
through the day,
just out of sight,
but always present.
My world shines
a little
brighter
because he's in it.
His voice
soothes me,
warms me,
surrounds me.
He's my
last thought
before I drift
off to sleep.
He stars in
every one
of my dreams.

He is my
everything.

Xtina Marie

The Words

The words
"I love you"
are spoken often.
So often
they begin to lose
their meaning.
When I whisper
those words to you,
my heart
is pounding
to the rhythm of
your heart.
My eyes
are clouded over
with the feelings
no other has ever
evoked in me.
My soul
is sighing because
it knows the meaning
of those words.
Finally.
When you speak

those same words
to me,
I hear your voice
and I feel
your words.
You needn't ever
tell me
"I love you" again.
For we have made them
more than words.

Antiquing

You once jokingly
told me
we might grow
bored.
That there might
come a day
when we'd
have nothing more
to talk about
but antiquing.
I laughed
thinking that day
would never come.
I contemplate it
often.
As the minutes
turn into
hours
and I'm still
captivated
by your every word.
As the days turn into
weeks

and I'm more
in love with you
now than when
things were new
and shiny.
As the months turn into
years
and I can't imagine
a life without you in it.
Someday
we may talk
of antiquing.
And on that day
antiquing
will no longer be
boring.

Xtina Marie

Little Things

It's the
little things.
Sun bathing
on an old
blanket
threadbare
but soft,
while
tapping my foot
to the beat
of the drums
from some
90's grunge song
I still know
all the words to.
It's the
little things.
Feeling the warmth
of the breeze
gliding over
my skin,
kissing me
here— where

my skirt rides
high on my thighs
and there— where
my exposed navel
peaks through
because of a
missed button
on my over-sized
blouse.
It's the
little things.
Laughing at
stories
as I reminisce
with an old lover
and the warmth
it brings
to my heart
to hear
he never
stopped loving me.
It's the
little things.

Xtina Marie

The Rain

The sun
slipped behind
a cloud
and I couldn't help
but remember
walking hand-in-hand,
strolling aimlessly
through the
neighborhood,
a lifetime ago.
The sky
grew darker,
the wind
picked up,
and finally the rain fell.
I started
to run for home
when you
grabbed my arm
pulling me close
and kissed me
in the rain.

Time Clouds Our Memories

Why
is it when
I think back
to us
I remember only
the good parts?
I seem to forget
the fights,
the crying,
the hole in the wall,
the lonely nights
I'd fall asleep
with you in the
next room,
feeling so alone.
But no,
I remember
walking our dog
in the Florida sun.
Trips to the library
when we were too

broke for a real date.
Pizza and movie nights
on Wednesday.
Making love
more often
than we didn't.
I suppose
time clouds our memories
or maybe
there was always
more good
than there was
bad.

The What Ifs

What ifs
and shoulda
woulda couldas
haunt us
all the time.
What happened to him?
What if
he were the one
who got away?
Where would we be
if we'd stayed
together?
Better off?
Worse?
Does it even
matter
anymore?
But what if
it does?
What if
"Meant to be"
will always
find a way?

What if
"True love"
never really
dies?
I ask myself these
questions
as I dial his
cell
and wait
for him
to answer.

My Eyes

I walk
softly,
carefully
between
the headstones,
pausing occasionally
to read
an intriguing
epitaph.
Loving sister,
mother, daughter.
And I
wonder
did she have
blue eyes,
perhaps hazel,
like mine.
What color
was her hair?
Was it
curly
or straight?
Someday

Xtina Marie

will some
stranger
run their hand
over the
cool marble
of my headstone
and wonder
what color
my eyes
were?

True Love Never Really Dies

Will you cry
when I tell you
it's over?
Or will a
part of you
be relieved
you didn't
have to break
my heart?
Will you
miss me
when I'm gone?
Or will you
revel in
the silence
my absence
creates?
Will a tear slip
from the corner
of your eye
when I close the door

for the very last time?
Or will you
smile and
remember
all the love
we once shared
and tell yourself
true love
never really
dies?

Spring Cleaning

Windows open
breeze blowing
through
the house.
The smell of
the neighbor's
barbeque mixed with
off brand PineSol.
Cleaning,
sweating,
parting with this
and that.
As my mind
works out
the things
it knows
it needs
to part with.

Xtina Marie

So Ready

You always know
just what will
get me going.
A whispered word
here,
a slide of your hand
there.
And I'm already
so ready;
hot,
wet,
needy.
I respond
with breathy moans,
hardened nipples,
a spreading of
my legs,
a warm hand
wrapping around
you,
but you're already
so ready.

Breakup Song

You asked me
why
you'd never given me
a breakup song.
Maybe it was
because
life would
always
lead me back
to you.
Perhaps
our hearts
just knew
we were never
truly over.
We may need
a new love song
but we'll never need
a breakup song.

Xtina Marie

Like a Summer Afternoon

You taste like
a summer afternoon,
and the burst of flavor
on my tongue
as I bite into a grape,
it's tantalizing
juices
dribbling down
my chin.

Again

When it's late
and it seems
like there's
nothing
left in the world
but you,
I think
I may just
love you.
When I laugh
so suddenly,
the emotions
overtake me,
warming my heart,
I think
I may just
love you.
When the
hormones
flood my system,
sending me on
a high
like nothing I've ever felt,

I think
I may just
love you.
When those words
almost slip
and I want to say them
to you,
I know
I've fallen in love
with you.
Again.

One Day

One day
I won't just wish
to be kissing you.
I'll roll over,
snuggle close
and seek out your lips.
One day
I won't just wish
to be in your arms.
I'll go to you,
whisper in your ear,
and tell you
that I want to be held.
One day
I won't grab my phone
when I want to talk to you.
I'll turn to you
and I'll tell you
what's on my mind.
One day
our future
will be before us.

Xtina Marie

No more wishing
on the stars.
Until that day,
I'm content to spend
every moment with you
planning
our one day.

My Quirks

I overthink
everything.
I second guess myself
often.
I read between lines
that aren't
even there.
I'm jealous.
I'm insecure.
I blather
when I'm nervous.
I'm scattered.
I'm whimsical.
Rarely practical.
I'd much rather
put off something
if I can
do it tomorrow.

But…

I love hard.
Unconditionally.

Blindly.
Consumingly.
So, I may
drive you insane
with my quirks,
but when I tell you
I love you,
believe
I will love you
with all of
my heart.
Unconditionally.
Blindly.
Consumingly.

Forever.

Bared to Him

I am bare to him.
Exposed.
Vulnerable.
My skin
still wet—
glistening,
from the bath
that he drew.
I shudder out
a breath
as he whispers
in my ear,
his beard
rough
on my tender skin.
I feel him slide
his fingers over
my body
as he slides
the towel
from my form,
and he tells me
all of the dirty,

wicked,
wanton
things that he
wants to do
to me.
I shiver
but it's no longer
from the
cooling bath;
my soul
is bared to him.
Exposed.
Vulnerable.
I close my eyes
and just
feel.

You've Always Been Home

We are
connected.
Intertwined.
Linked.
Tangled.
Your soul whispers
to me
before your lips
ever form
words.
My heart thrums
to the rhythm
of the blood
rushing through
your veins.
My thoughts
travel the miles
that separate us,
always searching for you
because you've always been
home.

Xtina Marie

Forever

I love him.
But those words
aren't enough.
They pale.
Come up short.
Are insufficient.
I search my mind
for better words,
something a bit—
more.
Something
that will
encompass
the depth of feelings
he invokes.
Something
that will convey to him
that this time—
this time is for
keeps.
This time is
forever.
Perhaps

instead of whispering
"I love you,"
I will, instead
whisper
"Forever."

Xtina Marie

Too Far Apart

I love
falling asleep
to the sound
of you breathing.
The soft
inhales
and quiet snores—
maybe a
mumbled word
I can't quite
make out.
I close my eyes
try to match
my breathing
to yours
and hope to meet you
in my dreams
because
even when
you are
but a breath away
we are still
too far

apart

Xtina Marie

His Fate

She told him
she'd follow him
into the next life.
That she'd always
be there
right by his side.
Come rain or sun
through thick and thin
she wasn't going anywhere
she promised this
to him.
So, he wasn't
one bit surprised
to see the face
that greeted him
when hell opened
it's gates.
He just grabbed
her hand
and lead her
into eternity.
She was always
his fate.

I Remember

I remember
the feel
of his arms.
The warmth
of his embrace.
The smell
of his cologne.
The scratch
of his beard.
The safety
I felt
snuggled close.
Breathing
him in.
I remember
him.

Xtina Marie

Yours

Whisper
in my ear
all the
dirty things
you want to do
to me.
Mark me.
Bruise me.
Spank me.
Take me,
I'm yours
to do with
as you please.
My uneven gasps.
My warmth that
surrounds you.
My trembles
when I lose control.
My sweet
"I love you"
as I lie there
satisfied.
Satiated.

Complete.
I'm yours;
Do with me
what you please.

Xtina Marie

Come Sit with Me

Come sit with me,
watch the grass
grow.
Watch the paint
dry.
Listen to the
nothing
that surrounds us.
The beating of
my heart
that beats only
for you.
Let me
bear your
burden,
carry your
cross,
let me
soothe
your soul.
Come sit with me
as the day
turns into night.

As the nights
turn into weeks.
As the months
turn into years.
As the years
turn into
forever.
Come sit with me.

Craziness

My heart
pitter pattered,
beat,
throbbed
in time
to the
craziness
he created in me.
A craziness
only he could
drum up.
A craziness
I hadn't felt
in decades.
A craziness
I never wanted
to let go.

He Says

He says
she makes him
smile.
Sing in
the shower
and want to
dance in
the rain.
He says
it's always
been her,
that she's
always been
the one.
When it's late
and he whispers
how much he loves her,
she knows
she's already smiling,
already singing
in the shower,
already dancing in
the rain.

Xtina Marie

And she knows
it's always
been him.

I Need Nothing

Each week
I drive past this
old trailer.
The porch
sags,
it's in dire need
of a fresh coat of paint.
The grass is slightly
overgrown
and the car in
the driveway
hasn't moved
in years.
Two rocking chairs,
side by side
no table in
between.
An old couple sit,
holding hands
even in the

July heat.
I make up
names for them
sometimes.
Is she an
Edith?
Maybe a Martha.
And he must be
Stanley. Perhaps
Phillip.
I wave
when I drive past
and hope someday
that is us.
Sitting side by side,
holding hands
even in the
July heat,
on a porch
that's seen
better days,
looking at a lawn
that we're too old

to properly
care for,
while everyday
is still perfect
because
I need nothing
but you.

Xtina Marie

Full Circle

They say
life comes around
full circle.
I remember
laughing with you,
as we lay on the floor
of a crappy apartment,
talking
late into the night.
I remember
wedding plans and
hearing you say those words.
I love you.
Those words that
never before
and never after
held as much
weight. As much
promise.
Now here we are.

Decades later.
Again.
Laughing
and talking
late into the night.
Wedding plans and
hearing you say those words.
You love me.
You've always loved me.
And I am
completed.
Life came around
full circle.

Xtina Marie

Nothing but You

I long
to be able to
express
exactly
what you mean
to me.
The depths
of my feelings,
the consuming
desire
you breathe
into me.
But the words
fail me.
Are inadequate.
Fall so short.
And instead
I find myself
wishing
you could peer

into my head,
into my heart,
where there are
no need of words.
Where in the silence
there is nothing
but you.
In the silence
there is
nothing
but
you.

Xtina Marie

Two Lost Souls

I croon along
To Pink Floyd,
wishing you were here.
Instead of
pushing the sadness
away—the melancholy—
I embrace it.
I tell myself
when next
you are in my arms,
when next
my lips press against yours
I will hold
on to you
as if my life
depended on it.
As if
I were drowning
and you were the
only one

to save me.
As if we weren't
two lost souls

Xtina Marie

Lies

The devil
whispers
sweet lies
that sound
like truth.
I want to believe him.
And a part
of me does.
Just because
he is the
Father of Lies
does not mean
he can never tell truths;
they are just half truths.
Pretty little
white lies
that I gobble up
greedily.
When you tell me
you love me,

he nods emphatically,
whispers to me
that, indeed
you do love me.
Of course you do.
Mostly.
Sometimes.
But you'll never
love me
enough
to not
love her.

Xtina Marie

Her Own Kind of Beautiful

She stood
in the middle of the room
surrounded by
the elite,
the popular,
all the girls
she always wished
she was.
All the girls
dressed the same,
their matching designer jeans
and expensive lip gloss;
the smell of strawberries
sickening, and overpowering.
But there she stood.
In her converse high-tops,
and gypsy skirt,
her hair flowing freely

down her back.
Not one of them—
not one of
the pretty people.
For she was far from pretty.
She was
extraordinary.
She was
beautiful.
And she
outshined them all.

Xtina Marie

Pinky Swear

Memories flood.
Late night talks
and long walks
pinky swears
and orange soda.
Going to sleep
in your arms,
head on your chest,
my hand not so
innocently roaming.
Your kisses,
intoxicating.
Your eyes
telling me
how much you love me.
But…
it's time now
for new
memories.
Cross my heart and

pinky swear.

Xtina Marie

Tragedy

Love is
a necessary tragedy,
but it's still
a work of art.
Even when it's
just a rough draft,
a first dress rehearsal,
or a pencil outline.
Does it matter much
what the outcome is?
A disturbing psychological thriller
that gives you the chills,
an off-broadway play
that no one has heard of,
an abstract drawing
you just don't connect with.
It's all needed
to fill the void,
to balance the scales,
to right the wrongs,

to make the world go 'round.
Love is necessary
even when it's
a tragedy.

Xtina Marie

Pretty Dead Thing

I watched the falling leaves.
But it was only August,
still warm
and muggy.
No autumn chill
in the air,
no electric snap
to the wind.
Just the
pretty dead things
falling,
scattering
on the lush
green grass.
A bit
out of place
with the sun
beaming down
and warming me.
And it occurred to me.

I was being prepared.
Prepared to say
goodbye to you.
Prepared to see
what once was
falling
and scattering—
once alive and so
exuberant
now just
a pretty dead thing.

Xtina Marie

Eternal Flame

Weak in the knees,
still begging you please
warm and wet
you'd slid in with ease.
Calling my name
as I do the same
this is more than mere lust,
my eternal flame.
I love you today
like I did yesterday.
My vow to you;
this time I won't stray.

My Ashley
May 23, 1975- July 12, 2018

I was the good girl
who wanted to
be bad
but was afraid.
I tried my first cigarette
with Ashley
in the girl's bathroom
between classes.
She blew
smoke rings
while I
coughed, but still
she never laughed.
Sitting behind me
in history class,
she pierced my ears
while I tried
not to flinch
even as a
drop of blood
splashed the collar

of my white blouse.
At that little bar
across the street from
the dumpy apartment
she called home,
she taught me how
to throw a dart,
how to hold
a pool stick
and what beer tasted like.
I still can't hit the
bullseye,
or the cue ball
and the taste of beer
still makes me gag.
But every time
I wear earrings,
I think of
Ashley.

Calloused Fingers

Paint me a picture
with the words
you whisper in my ear
as if you held
a Blick in your hand;
those masculine
calloused fingers
I long to intertwine
with my own.
Inscribe for me
a poetic work
of art
that would rival
the greats;
a Keats or Browning,
perhaps even Shakespeare.
Make me yearn
for the worn words
between the yellowed pages
of the dusty book
tucked away in the back
of the used bookstore

on Main
as your calloused fingers
reach for
that same volume.

on Main

The First Sip

You were my first
sip of champagne
sitting across
the glass coffee table
when we were
still in our teens.
I gazed at you,
as I brought
the flute to my lips
and I wondered
what you'd
taste like.
Would you
burst onto my tongue;
refreshing, bubbly?
Immediately
I was giddy.
Already drunk
on you

Xtina Marie

Unapologetically You

Laughing
at your own
jokes,
proud to call yourself
a nerd,
not caring what anyone
thinks;
you're
unapologetically you.
You love Jesus
but cuss a little,
drive the speed limit
in your sports car,
wear your hair long
with your ear pierced;
you're
unapologetically you.
You love video games,
and auto auctions
80's hair bands
and me
and I'll forever be

unapologetically
yours

Xtina Marie

Aftermath

Sweat beads
between
our naked bodies,
glistening
in the aftermath
of our love.
Breathing
Labored
I reach
to turn the fan on
the highest setting,
laughing, still trying
to catch my breath.

A Summer Night

Soon
so soon
the leaves will fall,
the air will chill,
the days will shorten.
Summer
will be
forgotten
almost as if
it had never
been.
Summer
will be
but a distant memory—
something
we only think of
fleetingly
when the nights
are cold and lonely.
Never forget.
I love you
like I love

Xtina Marie

a summer night.

I Hope

Shhh…
She might hear you
talking to me.
Late into
the night,
our whispers
quiet
but resounding
in the dead silence.
My heartbeat
echoing
off the still walls
pounding to the beat
of yours.
Stolen kisses,
breathy sighs
whispered words
of love
I hope are
only for me.
I hope.

Xtina Marie

Time Flies

Time flies.
Memories
of the past
haunt.
Birthdays
and blowing out candles,
chocolate cake and presents.
Easter Sundays,
Sunrise service,
pastel dresses and
patent leather mary janes.
Summers
playing in the sun,
slumber parties
and water parks.
Back to school shopping,
first crushes
best friends and detention.
Winters
and trimming trees,
candy-filled stockings
and Christmas music.

Time flies.
Boyfriends
then marriage,
babies and a mortgage.
The family dog dies,
the kids move away,
the house is empty, quiet.
Looking back
the only constant being
Time, and me.

A perfect day
to go walking
in the rain.

Xtina Marie

Still

I can still feel
the scratch
of your beard,
your breath
on my neck
and your taste
in my mouth.
The touch
of your
calloused fingers
plays on repeat
in my mind.
I can still hear
the whispered
"I love you,"
and your
sigh of pleasure
as you take me
over the edge
yet again.
I can still recall
the feel of your heart

beating wildly
against my ear,
your skin slick
with a light coat
of sweat
and your hair
grazing my cheek.
Bringing my hand
to my mouth
I touch my lips
swollen
from your kisses—
Still

Xtina Marie

Nashville

I left my heart
in
Nashville.
There in the
parking lot
of the hotel
as I
watched
you pull away.
Had you
looked
in the rearview mirror
perhaps
you'd have seen
me break down;
the sobs
that wracked my body.
Perhaps
you would have
turned around.
Perhaps
you would have

taken me
in your arms
and never
let me go.
Perhaps.

Xtina Marie

October Kisses

I walk the streets
early November
cold, wet leaves
of all colors
scatter and crunch
underfoot.
That song—
The one from that 90's band—
about heart's changing
and candles
in the November rain
flit through
my mind
and all I can think about
is you.
For years to come
I will recall
this walk,
the feel of
your warm lips
against mine,
and I'll know

it was you
who kept me warm
with your
October kisses.

Xtina Marie

Letting Go

When it's good—
it's great.
You mesh.
Connect.
Talk all hours
of the day and night.
Make love
with a passion
you swear
you've never felt
before.
You laugh
'til you see tears.
Your thoughts
forever them.
And then…
You fight
more often than you
fuck.
You make
excuses—
Say you're too busy

because
you'd rather
paint your nails
than argue
on a Saturday night
that used to be date night.
You no longer mesh.
No longer connect.
No longer laugh—
the tears
are painful now.
Can we fix
what's been broken?
Do we even want to?
You wonder
what would hurt more—
continuing this
or letting go?

Xtina Marie

In the World

I love the way
he looks at me
when he thinks
I'm not looking.
He has this
ability
to make me feel
like the only
woman
in the room—
the only woman
in the world.
And when we're
together
there is nothing left;
his fingers
link with mine,
his lips find me,
our heart beats
become one
and we're the only lovers
left

in the world.

Xtina Marie

Robin

My early 20's
were spent
partying
with you.
Climbing over
the stall in the
bathroom
at the local bar
just because
I'd never done it
Before.
Singing loudly
and off key
to that Eagles song
they played
at least
twice a night.
I was so drunk
that one time
I chucked popcorn
on your neck
from the backseat

of some
beat up car
and you laughed
'til I was sure
we'd crash.
That's probably
my best memory
of you and one
I will take with me
from here on.
Your laughter.
You always—
always
found a reason
to laugh.

You will be in my heart forever. I love you,
Robin. Give my mom a big hug from me.

Even when

we're touching
you're too far away.

Xtina Marie

Home

I drifted
lost my way
for too long
and
didn't think
I'd ever find
my way back.
All it took
was a touch
a whisper
a sigh
and
I am home
grounded
stable
safe and secure
in your arms
always.

He's Beautiful

He's
beautiful
but he
doesn't see it,
and I can't help
but sneak glimpses
when I don't think
he knows.
The way his eyes
crinkle
at the corners;
that sexy
wink
he doesn't even
realize
he's doing;
the curve
of his lips
when he
catches me
staring
and smiles.

Xtina Marie

He's
beautiful
and he
doesn't even
know it.

Your Lips

I could write
a whole book
on just
your lips.
How they softly
glide
over mine,
teasing lovingly
as I
open to you.
How they
graze
my ear
and leave me
shaking
with need.
How they
play
over my neck
sucking here—
and there

'til I can't quite
recall
my own name
but can still
moan yours.
How they
seek
me out in
the dark,
kissing me
intimately
here—
and there
'til I am
covered in
sweat
and begging for
more.
I could write
a whole book
on just
your lips
and read
aloud

as you
inspire me.

Xtina Marie

Until You

I never
understood
how two people
who claimed
to love
each other
crazily
madly
deeply
at one time
could be so
vile
hateful
vindictive
when the
relationship died.
I never
understood
until you.
As I hear the
vicious

callous
cruel
venom spew from your lips
I finally
understand.

Damaged

He says I am
damaged
destructive
disastrous—
and he's
been working on
"fixing"
me, but I
never learn.
He says
maybe
I might be a little bit
cute
that I'd never be
beautiful—
but he'd lower his
standards
this once.
He says I am
airheaded
dizzy
should have been

a blonde
and that's why he was
condescending
at times.
You say I am
fascinating
funny
flirty
and you can't
get enough of me.
You call me
beautiful
desirable
sexy
and you can't
keep your hands
off of me.
You say I am
smart
opinionated
sassy
and you could
talk to me for hours.
Why do I have

such trouble accepting
your praise
but believe
all the negativity
he breathed?
Maybe
he was right
and I really am
Damaged.

You don't think
your
random acts of kindness
are anything
special
but they mean
so much
to me.

Linger

His touch
lingers
long after his hands
have drifted
to new
places.
His lips
follow,
blazing a trail
across
my skin.
Even when
we're touching
he's still
too far away

Xtina Marie

Sweet Nothings

I love
the early morning hours
lying in
your arms
as we talk quietly,
whispering
sweet nothings,
hands roaming
innocently
before the
sun
starts peeking through
the blinds,
pressed warmly
to your side
tracing
lazy circles
on your chest
as I listen
to your heartbeat,
matching my breathing
to yours,

sleepy
but not wanting
to sleep,
recalling
the words to
that Aerosmith song,
thinking
I don't
want to miss a thing.

Xtina Marie

The One

I don't need
a sparkly ring,
a fancy stained-glass
windowed church
or solemn vows
uttered before
some suited up
man of God
to know that
we're forever.
I feel it
in every brush
of your fingers
as you
reach for my hand
and the warmth
of your breath
on my cheek
as you drift off
to sleep.
I feel it

every time
you pull me close
for a kiss—
your lips moving
softly
over mine—
or your arms
wrap around me,
surrounding me
in your warmth.
I don't need
to stand before
our friends and family
and profess my
undying love to you—
I feel it on the air
in the breeze
and written in the
clouds.
You are
the one.

Run away
with me
to that cabin
in the mountains

of my dreams.

Xtina Marie

My All

No boundaries
no walls
I freely give you
my all
no lies
of omission
or avoiding
the truth
I place it
before you
standing tall
we're a team
you and I
I'll help you walk
or help you crawl
in your arms
together
we'll always be
together
we can't fall

Lost

Often
she gets
lost
in her head
when the
music
is just right.
When Robert Plant
cries "Baby please
don't go,"
and
Steven Tyler
dreams on.
And she can't help
the melancholy
wash over as
David Gilmour
sings
about
fish and lost souls.

For 5 days
straight
my only friend;
the warm
faded blues
of the old
flannel nightgown
and my box of tissues.

The Next Chapter

You are
the protagonist
of your own
story.
Be the
heroine,
the savior,
the survivor
not the
villain,
the demon,
the victim.
When they
tell you
you can't—
prove you will.
When they think
the story's over
write the
next chapter.

Xtina Marie

I Wish You Well

Even though
our end was rough
and we both
said
some things
better left
unsaid—
I wish you well.
Even though
I never meant
to hurt you
and at times
it seemed
that was
your goal—
I wish you well.
Even though
you were
everything
for so long
and you
always

always
told me
this wasn't real—
I wish you well.
Even though
I still flinch
when someone
says your name—
I wish you well.

Xtina Marie

I Am Yours

I've been a bad girl.
Spank me.
Make me count
as you
turn my
ass cheeks
red and warm
to the
touch.
Grab me
by the hair
and force me
to my knees
as I'm already
dropping
before you.
Mark me
with little
love bites
all over my neck
so the world
knows

I am yours.

I am yours.

Xtina Marie

The Road Before Me

Flying
along the back roads
of Tennessee
in early February
the mountains
a picturesque
backdrop
top down
with the
sun warming
the goosebumps
on my arms
through the thin
material
of my favorite
black and white
sweater
all twists
and sudden turns

my stomach
dropping
when I can't
see the road
before me
gripping
your hand
tighter
I smile
leaning into
the next turn
trusting you to always
keep me safe

Xtina Marie

That Beauty

He tells me I'm
beautiful
while brushing
whisps of hair
from my face.
His eyes tell
the truth.
I am beautiful—
even with
no makeup,
messy hair,
in my favorite grey t-shirt
that frays at the bottom.
I catch
glimpses
in the mirror
as I pass by
and I start to see
that beauty.

Musty Romance Novels

Breathless
and needy
I shake
with the slide
of your hand;
hot and feverish
already
dripping
with desire;
on all fours
I give of myself
fully
trusting you
completely
as you take me
to heights
I've only read of
in dog-eared
musty

Xtina Marie

romance novels
in dimly lit corners
of used bookstores

He is Mine

He calls me
kitten
as he
buckles
my restraints
and leads me
by the
collar
to kneel
before him.
He calls me
his good girl
as I please him
with hands
securely
behind my back
mouth open
and ready.
He calls me
his
as he

marks me
and fills me
and I know by
his growls
of approval
he is
mine.

Tangle

I awoke
on a dark
rainy
Tuesday
in a
tangle
of blankets
arms
legs
surrounded by
your warmth
scent
masculinity
and I wanted
nothing more
than to
be lulled back
to sleep
by
your heart beats

Xtina Marie

Every Damn Day

You can make
reservations
at a 5 star restaurant
with a name
in some other
language
that I have trouble
pronouncing,
order
my favorite dish
and a bottle of
expensive wine—
the fruity kind
you know I fancy—
surprise me
with gourmet
chocolate truffles
I adore
maybe some flowers
and something
sparkly

to adorn my
neck
a
romantic card
or a soft
cuddly stuffed
animal
you caught me
ogling
at that
department store
we frequent.

But…
the truth is
I feel
your love for me
every day
every
damn
day
expressed more
strongly
when you

hold the
car door open
and cook dinner
if I'm busy.
When you
plug my phone in
at night
when I forget
and pour me
apple juice
when I'm sick.
When you
kiss me
and hold me
and whisper
"I love you."
I don't need
one day
a year
devoted
to lovers.
You give me
more than that
every day

every
damn
Day

Xtina Marie

Kiss

When you
kiss me
the whole world
stops
pauses
halts
as if
the universe
were
holding
it's breath
waiting
not able
to breathe
for fear
of missing out
on the
awesomeness
of that one
kiss

The Fantasy

Fantasy
is always better
than the
reality—
people say.
Possibly
those people
have never been
completely love-struck
smitten
utterly obsessed.
Face to face
we lie—
your hands
tracing
every inch of
my bared flesh,
your eyes
communicating
the words unspoken,
your kisses

Xtina Marie

becoming
frenzied
wild
feverish
 as desire—
the fire
smoldered within.
I am so
completely love-struck
smitten
utterly obsessed
with you
and the reality
far surpasses
the fantasy

Red Platform Heels

We stroll
through the mall
arm in arm
window shopping
smelling
the scented candles
and spritzing
the colorful bottles
of varying body mists.
He humors me
when I have to
try on
every shoe—
the sandals, the sneakers
even the boots.
Nodding toward
a red pair of platforms
he traces a
finger
down the shiny heel.
Giggling

Xtina Marie

I tell him
I'd break my neck
walking in those.
He winks—
that panty melting wink—
telling me
not to worry
I'll be
flat on my back
as he
carries the red platform heels
to the counter

Devotion

True desire
is
captivating
I thirst
for your
kiss
always hunger
for your
embrace
forever entranced
my devotion
is eternal

Xtina Marie

Kathleen

Poets
write for
themselves
random
words
bubbling forth
akin to
a fresh bottle
of champagne
uncorked.
Poets
feel the words
tasting them—
some sweet and beautiful
while others
bitter and painful—
long before
the ink
ever blemishes
the paper.
Poets

touch lives
around them
unaware
without intent
never learning
Kathleen
was moved to
tears.
Poets
immortalize
life
see things
differently
through
distinct glasses
sometimes
rose colored
other times
black and harsh.
I lift my
flute in a toast
as I touch
my pen to
my bottom lip

and think of
Kathleen.

For 5 Straight Days

It's been
raining
now
for 5
straight days
all I want
to do
is cuddle
with you
forget
the world
and just
breathe

Xtina Marie

That Beautiful Town

It rained
continuously
in Gatlinburg
yet we still
strolled
hand in hand
down the strip
enjoying
attractions
but I suspect
you paid
more attention
to my eyes
lighting up
at the penguins
and when I tried
fondue
for the first time
than anything
in that beautiful town

That Ass

"That ass
is mine,"
he says and
swats me
when I'm in
reach
the contact
the sting
the heat
lights
my face in
a smile
the contact
the sting
the heat
sparkle
his eyes
animalisticly
hedonisticly
that ass
is his

Xtina Marie

The Train

She was
always
the little
engine
that could
never giving up
never outta
steam
kept chugging along
accepting what was
without complain
'til the day
she stopped
stood up
decided
she no longer
needed
to go with the
flow
so
she became
the train

Seconds Before

The contrast
pleasure and pain
drives me
while I
squeal
and
jump
with the
crack
of the paddle
and the
pain
that washes
fluidly
in the same
manner
as an orgasm
I wait
in impatient
anticipation
for your
soft caress
and feathery

Xtina Marie

kisses
upon the
same skin
you marred
only
seconds before

We're Gonna Fight

We're gonna
fight
one day
I might
say something
that pisses
you off
or forget
to wash the clothes
when you've reminded me
a million times
that all of your
socks
are dirty
maybe
you'll forget
to rinse the
bathroom sink
after
you shave
or pay too much
attention

to your phone
while I sit
silently
begging
for you to
look my way
you get
cranky
when you're
hungry
and I get
whiny
when I'm tired
I promise
swear
vow
to never
close my eyes
for the
night
with anger
in my heart
if you
promise
swear
vow

to always
wake
with a
kiss
on your lips
for only
me

Xtina Marie

Safe Word

I love
all the
kinky
games
we play
when you
tell me
I'm your
dirty girl
and slap me
on the ass
when you
grab
my hair
and guide me
by force
and I'm
wondering
if I'll remember
the safe word
should I
need it

Clichés

My heart's
been broken
or ripped
in pieces
such
clichés
overused
abused
generically
tossed about
so often
their meaning
is unfelt
lost
unappreciated.
I ponder
the accuracy
of these phrases
carefully—
patting
my chest
I can
assure you

Xtina Marie

my heart
resides
where it's
meant
and that
the pieces
are intact
I assure you this
laying
in a heap
on the floor
watching
the beige carpet
turn crimson
with my blood
while I clutch
the broken
shards
of your
picture
to my
aching chest

Speechless

Be careful
heed
consider
the
empty words
the
vain platitudes
we spew forth
daily
the
eternal vows
we toss
to and fro
while we flit
about aimlessly
from
this or that
eventually
a moment arises
fervent
profound
magical
that we'll

Xtina Marie

seek
to express
describe
but we've
strewn
scattered
such
meaningless
nonsense
we're left
speechless

In the Movies

You know those
scenes
in the movies
where
the hero
kisses the heroine
and leaves her
flustered
breathless
shaky
and you roll
your eyes
because
that doesn't really
happen
not in
real life
not in
your life
then
he kisses you
and you
forget

your name

192

The Submissive

Devotedly
by your
side
I stand
following
your lead
trusting
your guidance
abandoning
my worries
obediently
at your
feet
I kneel
awaiting
your direction
needing
your attention
seeking
your approval

Xtina Marie

Silence

Communication
is key
we say
while we sit
an arm length
away
in silence
wondering
what the
other
is thinking
is he
mad at me
is he just
tired
from a
long day
is there
something
troubling
on his mind
he's not
shared with

me
what's wrong
inside
I'm screaming
but he
can't hear
a thing
I'm
thinking
yet
I still
sit
an arm length
away
in silence

Xtina Marie

Spring Wafts

The smell
of spring
wafts
through
open windows
fluttering
the sheers
with the
aroma of
burgers
on the grill
and the promise
of lazy
nights
sitting out
on the balcony
watching the
fireflies

The Photo

At his
day job
with the window
overlooking
a busy street
noisy
even in
the dead of night
or before
the sun
peeked above
the horizon
his head
a fog
always on
autopilot
he fingers
the old photo
he found
while
cleaning out
his grandfather's
belongings

Xtina Marie

a month
after
the funeral
when the
wound was still
so fresh
black and white
worn
images
of a time
long past
a time
forgotten
impatient honking
from the
street below
interrupts
his thoughts
and he tucks
the photo
in the pocket
of his tailored
suit jacket
until
the next time
he can

pull it out
and daydream
about
a life
gone
but never
forgotten

Xtina Marie

I Get Lost

I get
lost
in your
kisses
and the
swirl
of your
tongue
against mine
while
time stops
I am
found
in your
touch
as your
hand glides
and your
fingers
search out
the places

radiating
heat
from the
desire
that burns
within me
I'm blinded
by the
passion
of the blood
roaring
through
my veins
but now
I see
through
the love-induced
haze
that lights
a fire
connecting
our hearts
our souls
our lives

Xtina Marie

**I get
lost**

I get

They Say

She's
so strange,
they say
and
they refuse
to invite her
to join their
little clique
she dresses
so weird,
they whisper
when they
catch sight of her
on the street
outcast
abnormal
freak
words
flung
in her direction
here

and there
they are so
full of
judgement
condemnation
clamor
but their
poison
is
only
killing
them

Big Apple Red

He paints my
toenails
Big Apple Red
and absently
tightens his grip
on my calf
while I run
my fingers through
his long hair
and daydream
shivering
from the
electricity
that pulses
through my body
from his touch

Xtina Marie

The Artist

she's
an artist
first
she
sees things
differently
than
most
she's
whimsical
and oft
times
she's
too busy
looking
at the sky
instead
of the world
around her
he was
always

trying to
fix
change
modify her
'til she
realized
it wasn't
her
that needed
fixing
changing
modifying
she's
an artist

About the Author

The Accidental Poet:

Xtina Marie is an avid horror and fiction genre reader, who became a blogger; who became a published poet; who became an editor; who now is a podcaster, and an aspiring novelist—and why not? People love her words.

Her first book of poetry, Dark Musings has received outstanding reviews in addition to being nominated for a Bram Stoker Award for poetry. It is likely she was born to this calling. Writing elaborate twisted tales to entertain her classmates in middle school would later lead Xtina to use her poetry as a private emotional outlet in adult life—words she was hesitant to share publicly—but the more she shared, the more accolades her writing received.

Her first romance erotica novel is well under way but has taken a back seat to an ever-increasing number of commitments.

Xtina has been published in numerous anthologies and now has 3 poetry books under her belt; Dark Musings, Light Musings and Darkest Sunlight.

OTHER POETRY FROM HELLBOUND BOOKS
www.hellboundbookspublishing.com

Darkest Sunlight

"The heart was made to be broken." - *Oscar Wilde*

To allow your heart to soar, you must risk the depths. Darkest Sunlight is the third poetic narrative from Xtina Marie. In this journey, readers will begin in the darkest of places yet revealed to us by this critically acclaimed poet, only to then find themselves thrust into the brightness of love before their eyes and minds can fully adjust. It is this shocking contrast which best conveys what it is to love, lose, and love again.

In Dark Musings, Xtina explored sadness. In Light Musings, she explored the intricacies of a loving heart. In Darkest Sunlight, Xtina Marie compares the opposite ends of the spectrum, and in doing so, she found a place darker than black.

<u>Dark Musings</u>

The perfect companion piece to Light Musings – The dark side of Xtina Marie's poetry delves into intense emotions: heartache, loss, hurt, pain, rage, and a dangerous consuming love which can drive one insane. Dark Musings is not a collection!

The author returned to the centuries old practice of Narrative Poetry—the telling of a story through poetry. If you believe you are brave enough to explore the savage emotions of the human heart; Dark Musings will test your mettle.

<u>Light Musings</u>

The perfect companion piece to Dark Musings – an intriguing mirror image of the darkness you have just read, but no less deep and soul stirring.

What a web she weaves. Light Musings is a poetic narrative—a story told through related poems. Xtina Marie is a master of this style. Known by her fans as the Dark Poet Princess, this term of endearment came about as a result of the horror genre embracing her first book: Dark Musings which continues to garner stellar reviews. Light Musings will not disappoint her loyal fans as darkness is present within these pages as well. However, this latest book will show a much larger audience that Xtina's poetry pulls out every feeling the reader has ever experienced—forcing them to feel with her protagonist. Light Musings shows us that love is made from darkness and light; something Xtina Marie explores like no one else.

Gray Skies of Dismal Dreams

Prepare for an excursion into a gloomy world of shadows, where the days are never sunlit and blithe, and where the nights are wrapped in endless nightmares.

No happy endings or silver linings are found in the clouds that fill these gray skies.

But what you will find, gathered in one volume, are the darkest of poems and tales of horror, waiting to take your mind on a journey into realms of the uncheerful and the unholy.

An amazingly surreal collection of short stories and the darkest of poetry, all interspersed with stunning graveyard photographs taken by the multitalented author herself - an absolute must for every bookshelf!

Beautiful Tragedies

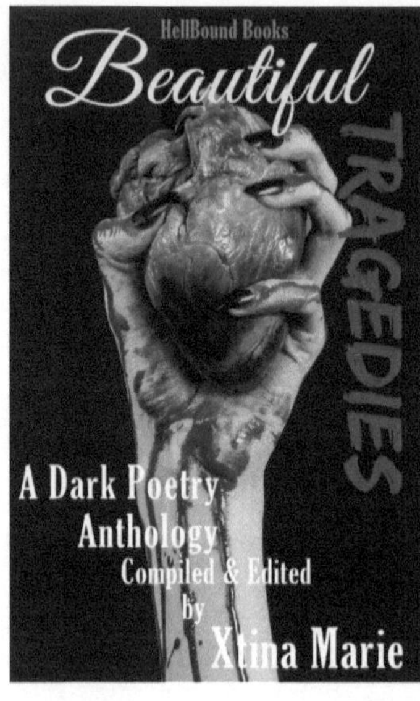

Only through dark poetry can a tragedy become something truly beautiful.

"Beauty is in the eye of the beholder." This phrase has origins dating back to ancient Greece, circa 300 BC; proving that some humans have always had the ability to see beauty where others could not.

Beautiful Tragedies is a compilation of 140 works by no less than fifty-five amazing poets writing in a variety of forms--all inspired by feelings born in the darkest of times.

Detours and Dead Ends

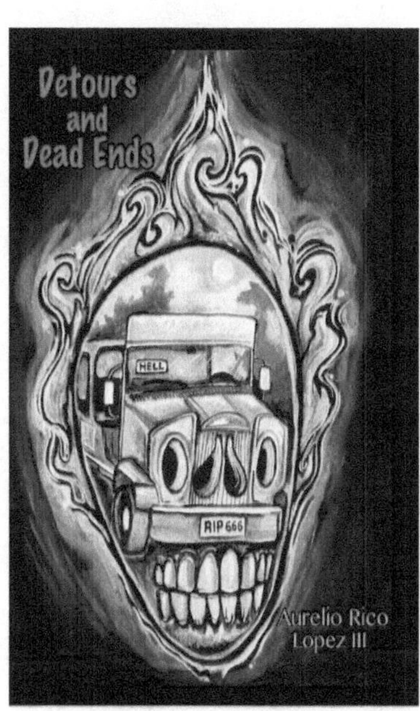

There are so many poems that invoke feelings of romance, wonderment, and joy.

These aren't them.

Aurelio Rico Lopez III is an exceedingly talented writer and poet who manages to conjure up scenes of mayhem, fear, and cosmic dread in this poetry collection, Detours and Dead Ends.

Lopez brings a bit of artistic flare to his signature style of writing and provides a book that takes the reader from murder to revenge, from unfortunate circumstances to several different flavors of the apocalypse.

So crack it open and enjoy the ride..

Tripping Balls

A thought provoking, eclectic, disturbing and at times downright weird collection of poetry, short stories and insightful musings from the inimitable Gocni Schindler....

He offers a variety of stories which beautifully gives the awesome reader, like you, the opportunity to experience different levels of thought and contemplation. I know, it's so exciting! God willing, some humor as well.

**A HellBound Books LLC
Publication**

www.hellboundbookspublishing.com

Printed in the United States of America

www.ingramcontent.com/pod-product-compliance
Lightning Source LLC
Chambersburg PA
CBHW050525190726
48284CB00003B/938